IF
I RAN
the CIRCUS

如果我来经营
马戏团

[美]Dr. Seuss 图文
薛振冰 译

中国出版集团
中国对外翻译出版公司

图书在版编目（CIP）数据

如果我来经营马戏团/(美)苏斯著；薛振冰译–北京：中国对外翻译出版公司，2007.1
（苏斯博士双语经典）书名原文：If I Ran the Circus
ISBN 978-7-5001-1716-2

I.如… II.①苏…②薛… III.①英语–汉语–对照读物②童话–美国–现代 IV. H319.4：I

中国版本图书馆 CIP 数据核字 (2006) 第 142729 号

（著作权合同登记：图字 01-2006-7167 号）

出版发行 / 中国对外翻译出版公司
地　　址 / 北京市西城区车公庄大街甲 4 号物华大厦六层
电　　话 / (010)68359376　68359303　68359101　68357937
邮　　编 / 100044
传　　真 / (010)68357870
电子邮箱 / book@ctpc.com.cn
网　　址 / http://www.ctpc.com.cn

策划编辑 / 李育超　薛振冰　王晓颖
责任编辑 / 李育超
特约编辑 / 王甘
责任校对 / 韩建荣　卓玛
英文朗读 / Rayna Martinez & Camila Tamayo
封面设计 / 大象设计

排　　版 / 翰文阳光
印　　刷 / 北京画中画印刷有限公司
经　　销 / 新华书店

规　　格 / 787×1092 毫米　1/16
印　　张 / 4.5
字　　数 / 20 千字
版　　次 / 2007 年 4 月第一版
印　　次 / 2007 年 5 月第二次
印　　数 / 10 001-15 000

ISBN 978-7-5001-1716-2　定价：18.60 元

音频下载：登录 http://www.ctpc.com.cn 点击"苏斯博士双语经典"。

　　本书采用了隐形码点读技术，页码所在的椭圆部分置入了隐形码，可
配合爱国者点读笔产品点读发音。

谨以此书献给我的父亲，斯普林菲尔德的大特德，他是我所认识的最好的人。

★二十世纪最卓越的儿童文学作家之一
★一生创作48种精彩绘本
★作品被翻译成20多种文字和盲文
★全球销量逾2.5亿册
★曾获得美国图画书最高荣誉凯迪克
　大奖和普利策特殊贡献奖
★两次获奥斯卡金像奖和艾美奖
★美国教育部指定的重要阅读辅导读物

Adults are just obsolete children
and the hell with them.

大人都是些退化了的
孩子，让他们见鬼去吧。
——苏斯博士

苏斯是谁？

　　苏斯博士的图画书有着典型的个体化风格，明亮的色彩、简洁的线条、夸张的造型，配合原创的动画形象以及曲折、生动、紧凑的故事，使得画面和文字都呈现出一种张力和个性，这也是他的作品倍受儿童欢迎的重要原因之一。

　　苏斯独特的风格也表现在故事构架上。许多故事情节均包含不断升级的夸张、狂想，形成一种典型的苏斯式情节模式。有人曾经以"吹气球"来形容苏斯博士讲故事的方式：他不断吹进空气，使得情节持续膨胀，几近爆破，等到读者快受不了了，期待气球"砰"的应声而破时，苏斯博士却又出乎意料——只是将气球放了气！另外，节拍明确有规律、易记易诵的韵文，更是苏斯式故事的显著标记。

　　在给孩子写写画画的大家里，苏斯博士肯定该归入一种另类。他完全把孩子当作大人一样看待，最大限度地"放纵"他们：让他们痛痛快快地"胡说八道"、"大闹天宫"。他甚至敢于激发他们潜意识中被压抑的自我，不惜以躁动不安作为代价。让孩子们从苏斯博士那里品味淋漓尽致的痛快吧，可是有一点要记住，千万不要在睡前讲！

"**I**n all the whole town, the most wonderful spot
Is behind Sneelock's Store in the big vacant lot.
It's *just* the right spot for my wonderful plans,"
Said young Morris McGurk, ". . . if I clean up the cans."

"在整个镇子里,最有趣的地方就是斯尼
洛克商店后面的这一大片空地了,这儿正好可
以实现我的宏伟计划,"小莫里斯·麦格克说,
"如果我把那些铁罐子清理出去……"

"Now a fellow like me," said young Morris McGurk,
"Could get rid of this junk with a half hour's work.
I could yank up those weeds. And chop down the dead tree.
And haul off those old cars. There are just two or three.
And then the whole place would be ready, you see..."

　　"像我这样的小伙子,半个小时就能把这些垃圾清理干净,"小莫里斯说,"拔掉杂草,砍倒枯树,再把那几辆破汽车拉出去。还好,只有两三辆。然后,整个地方就弄好了,你会看到……"

All ready to put up the tents for my circus.
I think I will call it the Circus McGurkus.

一切准备就绪，可以给我的马戏团把帐篷支
起来了。我想可以叫麦格克斯马戏团。

The Circus McGurkus! The World's Greatest Show
On the face of the earth, or wherever you go!

麦格克斯马戏团!世界上最伟大的表演!你能见到的最伟
大的表演!

The Circus McGurkus! The cream of the cream!
The Circus McGurkus! The Circus Supreme!
The Circus McGurkus! Colossal! Stupendous!
Astounding! Fantastic! Terrific! Tremendous!
I'll bring in my acrobats, jugglers and clowns
From a thousand and thirty-three faraway towns
To the place that you'll see 'em in, ladies and gents,
Right behind Sneelock's Store, in the Great McGurk tents!
And I don't suppose old Mr. Sneelock will mind
When he suddenly has a big circus behind . . .

麦格克斯马戏团!首屈一指的马戏团!麦格克斯马戏团!无与伦
比的马戏团!麦格克斯马戏团!阵容庞大!盛况空前!惊险刺激!其乐
无穷!惊心动魄!精彩绝伦!我要把杂技演员、魔术师和小丑全都带到
这里来,他们来自一千零三十三个遥远的小镇。女士们、先生们,你们
在斯尼洛克商店后面就可以见到他们,就在马戏团的帐篷里。我觉得
当斯尼洛克先生突然发现身后冒出来一个马戏团时,他是不会大惊小
怪的……

After all, Mr. Sneelock is one of my friends.
He might even help our doing small odds and ends.
Doing little odd jobs, he could be of some aid . . .
Such as selling balloons and the pink lemonade.
I think five hundred gallons will be about right.
And THEN, I'll be ready for Opening Night!

　　斯尼洛克先生毕竟是我的朋友,他也许还会帮上忙。做点儿小事情,他会帮上忙的……比如卖卖气球和粉色柠檬水。我觉得能装五百加仑的桶差不多就够了。然后,首演之夜就准备好了。

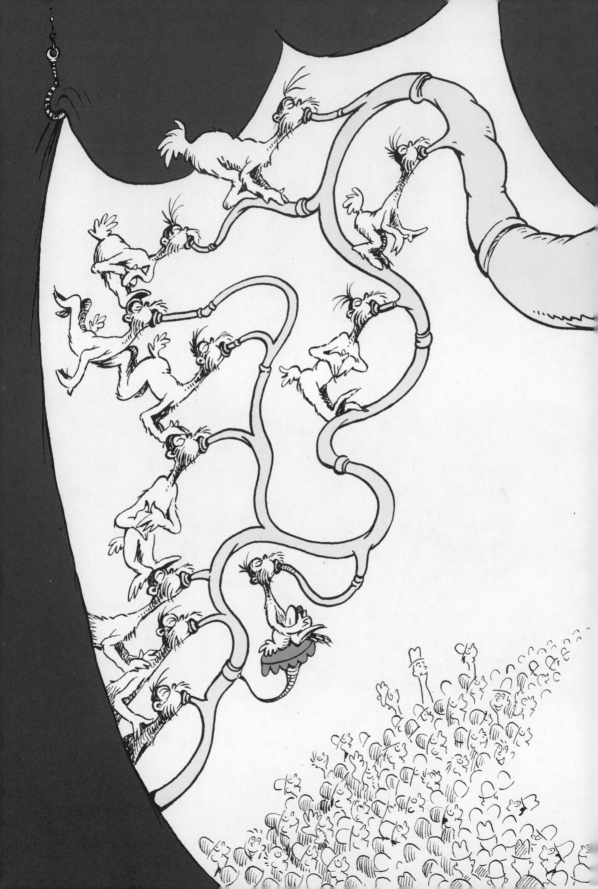

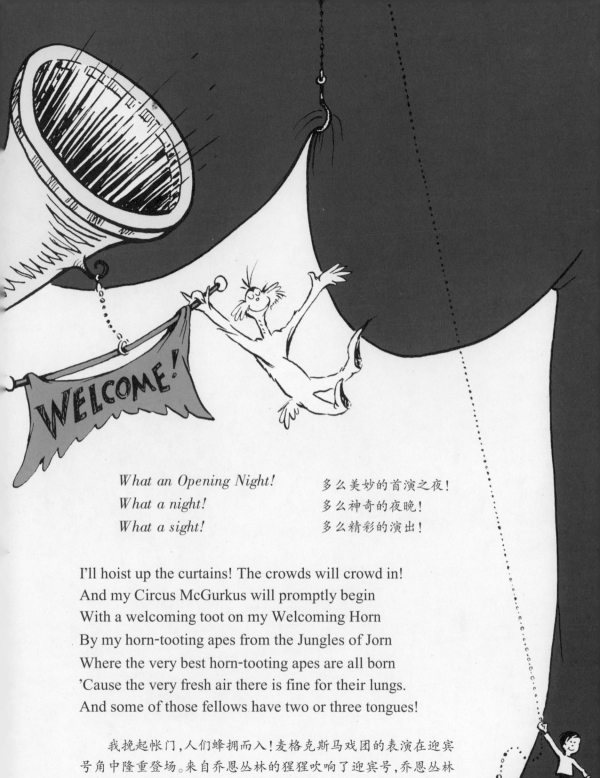

What an Opening Night!
What a night!
What a sight!

多么美妙的首演之夜！
多么神奇的夜晚！
多么精彩的演出！

I'll hoist up the curtains! The crowds will crowd in!
And my Circus McGurkus will promptly begin
With a welcoming toot on my Welcoming Horn
By my horn-tooting apes from the Jungles of Jorn
Where the very best horn-tooting apes are all born
'Cause the very fresh air there is fine for their lungs.
And some of those fellows have two or three tongues!

　　我挽起帐门，人们蜂拥而入！麦格克斯马戏团的表演在迎宾
号角中隆重登场。来自乔恩丛林的猩猩吹响了迎宾号，乔恩丛林
空气清新，有益肺部健康，有些猩猩长着两三个舌头呢！

This way! Step right in! This way, ladies and gents!
My Side Show starts here in the first of my tents.
When you see what goes on, you'll say no other circus is
Half the great circus the Circus McGurkus is.
Here on Stage One, from the Ocean of Olf
Is a sight most amazing—a walrus named Rolf
Who can stand on one whisker, this wonderful Rolf,
On the top of five balls! Two for tennis, three golf.
It's a marvelous trick, if I say so mysolf.

这边请!快进来!女士们、先生们,这边请!第一顶帐篷里表演的是些小节目。你要是看过这儿的演出,肯定会说其他的马戏团连麦格克斯马戏团的一半都赶不上。一号舞台上场的是一头名叫鲁尔夫的海狮,来自奥尔夫海,最令人惊讶的是他可以靠一根胡须倒立起来,身手不凡的鲁尔夫能立在五个球的顶上!两只网球,再加三只高尔夫球。要我说,这种本事真是不可思议。

And on Stage Number Two
Here is something quite new!

From a country called Frumm
Comes this Drum-Tummied Snumm
Who can drum any tune
That you might care to hum.
(Doesn't hurt him a bit
Cause his Drum-Tummy's numb.)

二号舞台上的表演令人耳目一新！

来自弗纳姆国的斯纳姆长了一个像鼓一样的肚子，他可以在圆鼓鼓的肚子上敲打出各种你喜欢的曲调。(他一点儿也不疼,因为他那圆鼓鼓的肚子已经麻了。)

And you'll now meet the Foon! The Remarkable Foon
Who eats sizzling hot pebbles that fall off the moon!
And the reason he likes them red hot, it appears,
Is he greatly enjoys blowing smoke from his ears.

　　你现在看到的是凡凡！凡凡可不同凡响，他能吃掉从月球上
落下来、烧得吱吱响的鹅卵石。他喜欢这些烧得红彤彤的东西，
因为他觉得从耳朵里往外喷烟其乐无穷。

Of course pebbles like this are quite hard to collect
But Sneelock will manage, somehow, I expect.
After all, Mr. Sneelock is one of my friends
And I'm sure he'll help out doing small odds and ends.

当然 , 这种石头很难搜集 , 不过 , 我想斯尼洛克会有办法的。
斯尼洛克毕竟是我的朋友 , 而且 , 我确信他会帮我这个忙。

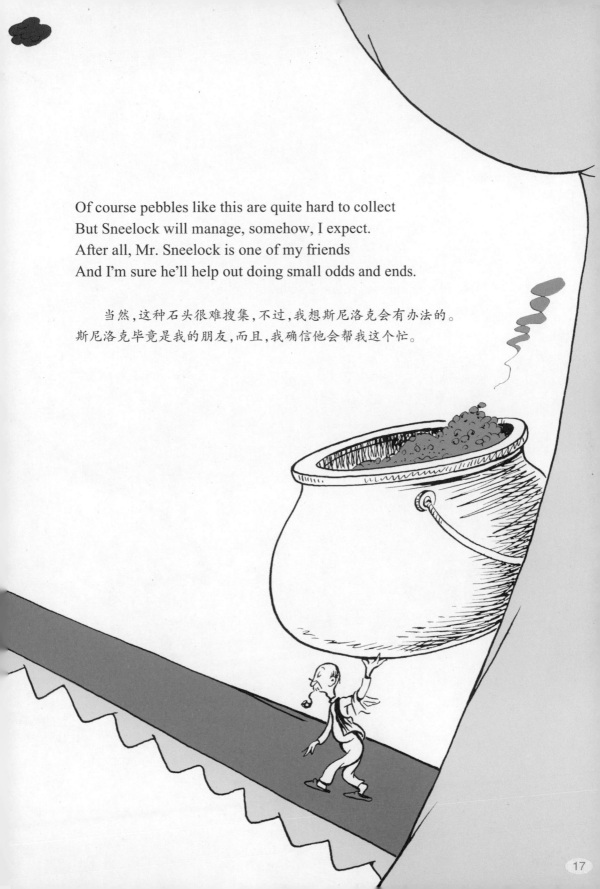

And on Stage Number Four, see the Wily Walloo
Who can throw his long tail as a sort of lassoo!
With a flip of the hip, with a tail of this kind
He can capture whoever is standing behind!
He can capture old Sneelock. I'm sure he won't mind.

在四号舞台上表演的是威利,他能把长长的尾巴甩成套索!
他只要一抖屁股,不管谁站在后面,他都能用尾巴套住!他能套
住老斯尼洛克。我确信,他不会介意的。

And now here is a Hoodwink
Who winks in his wink-hood.
Without a good wink-hood
A Hoodwink can't wink good.
And, folks, let me tell you
There's only one circus
With wink-hooded Hoodwinks!
The Circus McGurkus!

　　现在我们看到的是戴头罩的眨眼鸟，他在眨眼睛头罩里眨眼睛。要是没有个好的眨眼睛头罩，戴头罩的眨眼鸟就眨不好眼睛。朋友们，让我来告诉大家吧，只有一个马戏团有戴眨眼睛头罩的眨眼鸟，那就是麦格克斯马戏团！

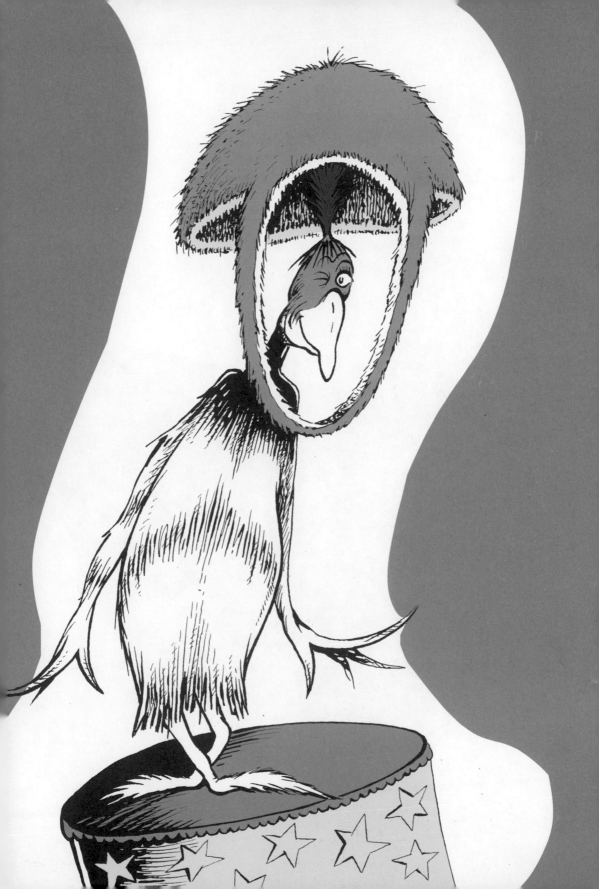

The Show of All Shows!
There's no other Showman
Who shows you a show with a Blindfolded Bowman!
The Blindfolded Bowman from Brigger-ba-Root,
The world's sharpest sharpshooter. Look at him shoot!
Through the holes in four doughnuts!
Two hairs on a worm!
And the knees of three birds
Without making them squirm!
And, then, on through a crab apple up on the head
Of Sneelock, who likes to help out, as I've said.

　　接下来可是顶极演出！让蒙住眼睛的弓箭手为大家表演，这样的马戏团的老板找不出第二个。蒙住眼睛的弓箭手来自布里格巴鲁特，是世界上最厉害的神箭手。瞧！他箭法多棒！穿过四个油炸圈饼！穿过毛毛虫的两根头发！从三只鸟的胯下飞过，他们竟然都纹丝不动！紧接着又穿过了斯尼洛克头顶上的山楂。我说过，斯尼洛克愿意帮忙。

And, now, come to this spot
Where the spotlight is hot
And you'll see in the spotlight
A Juggling Jott
Who can juggle some stuff
You might think he could not . . .
Such as twenty-two question marks,
Which is a lot.
Also forty-four commas
And, also, one dot!
That's the kind of a Circus McGurkus I've got!

现在,在耀眼的聚光灯下,你将看到玩杂耍的乔特,
他能耍一些你意想不到的东西,比如二十二个问号,这可
是个很大的数目。他还能耍出四十四个逗号,外加一个
句号!我的麦格克斯马戏团就是这样。

不过,这只是些小节目,只是个小小的序曲。这边是大帐篷,你会觉得头昏目眩。哎呀!女士们、先生们、孩子们、老人们,你们很快就会觉得脑袋转来转去,都要从肩膀上掉下来了!快!快点走!女士们、先生们,快!快到座位上去,这里是最华美的帐篷!最盛大的游行马上就要开始了!

But that's just my Side Show. A start. A beginning.
This way to the Big Tent! You'll find your head spinning.
Why, ladies and gentlemen, youngsters and oldsters,
Your heads will quite likely spin right off your shouldsters!
So hurry! Step lively! Quick, ladies and gents!
And get in to your seats in my Tent-of-all-Tents!
My Parade-of-Parades is about to commence!

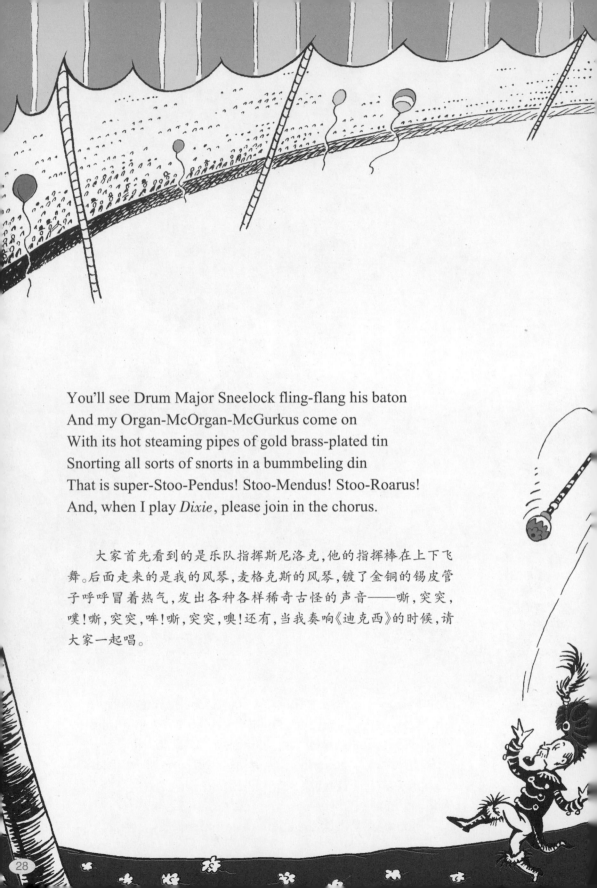

You'll see Drum Major Sneelock fling-flang his baton
And my Organ-McOrgan-McGurkus come on
With its hot steaming pipes of gold brass-plated tin
Snorting all sorts of snorts in a bummbeling din
That is super-Stoo-Pendus! Stoo-Mendus! Stoo-Roarus!
And, when I play *Dixie*, please join in the chorus.

大家首先看到的是乐队指挥斯尼洛克,他的指挥棒在上下飞舞。后面走来的是我的风琴,麦格克斯的风琴,镀了金铜的锡皮管子呼呼冒着热气,发出各种各样稀奇古怪的声音——嘶,突突,噗!嘶,突突,哗!嘶,突突,噢!还有,当我奏响《迪克西》的时候,请大家一起唱。

Then a fluff-muffled Truffle will ride on a Huffle

And, next in the line, a fine Flummox will shuffle.

The Flummox will carry a Lurch in a pail

And a Fibbel will carry the Flummox's tail

While, on top of the Flummox, three Harp-Twanging Snarp

Will twang mighty twangs on their Three-Snarper-Harp

While a Bolster blows bloops on a three-nozzled bloozer!

A Nolster blows floops on a one-nozzled noozer!

And *then* comes a lion who's partly a trout!

Then *more* stuff ! For forty-five minutes, about!

　　紧随其后的是戴着毛茸茸的头巾、骑在哈夫背上的塔夫，接下来是一只优雅的弗拉姆踱着方步。挂在弗拉姆肚子上的桶里坐着乐滋滋，菲宝在后面衔着弗拉姆的大尾巴，弗拉姆的背上还有三只弹竖琴的斯纳普，他们卖力地砰砰砰弹着三斯纳普竖琴，博斯特在旁边使劲儿吹着三管布鲁斯！诺斯特噗噗吹着单管努兹！再往后是一头狮子，长着鳟鱼的身子！后面还有很多！大约要四十五分钟。

And THEN, behind *them*, then,
While everyone stares
Come my To-an-Fro Marchers
Who march in five layers!
The Fros march on Tos
And the Tos march on Fros.
Don't know how they do it,
But that's how it goes.

　　他们后面的"来来往往"方阵让
每个人都瞠目结舌。这是一个五层方
阵!"往往"走在"来来"上面,"来来"
走在"往往"上面。真不知道他们是怎
么做到的,但他们确实在这样走着。

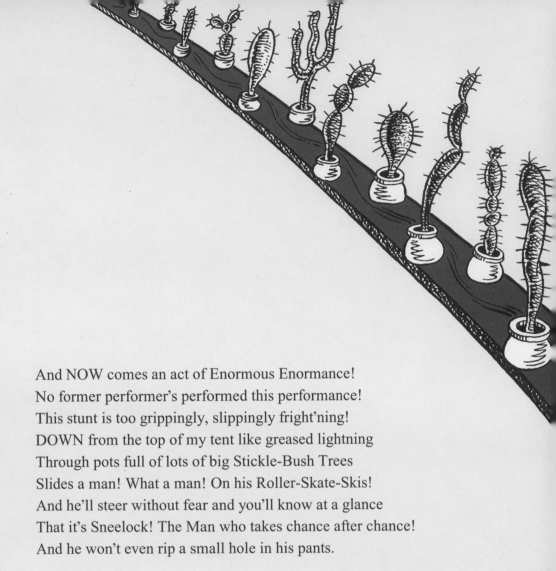

And NOW comes an act of Enormous Enormance!
No former performer's performed this performance!
This stunt is too grippingly, slippingly fright'ning!
DOWN from the top of my tent like greased lightning
Through pots full of lots of big Stickle-Bush Trees
Slides a man! What a man! On his Roller-Skate-Skis!
And he'll steer without fear and you'll know at a glance
That it's Sneelock! The Man who takes chance after chance!
And he won't even rip a small hole in his pants.

　　现在出场的是气势非凡的伊诺曼滑行表演!以前从来没有演员进
行过这样的表演!这种特技表演简直太引人入胜了,飞速滑行,惊险刺
激。他从我的帐篷顶上飞驰而下,像一道涂了润滑油的闪电,穿过那些
长满高大的针刺灌木的罐子!这个人真是胆略非凡!他脚踩滚轴雪橇,
一路驶来,面无惧色。你一眼就能认出来,是斯尼洛克!这个家伙一路上
险象环生!可是,他的裤子上连个小洞都没扎破。

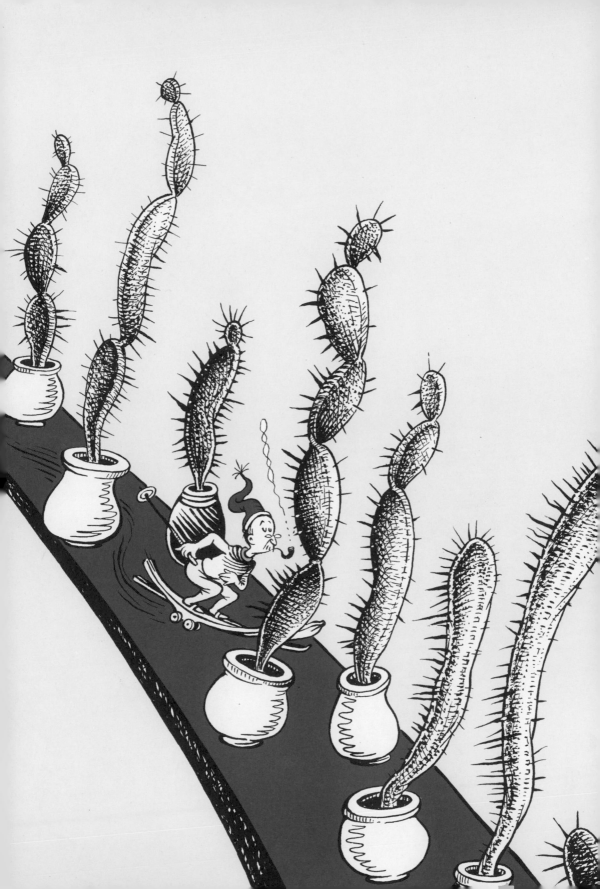

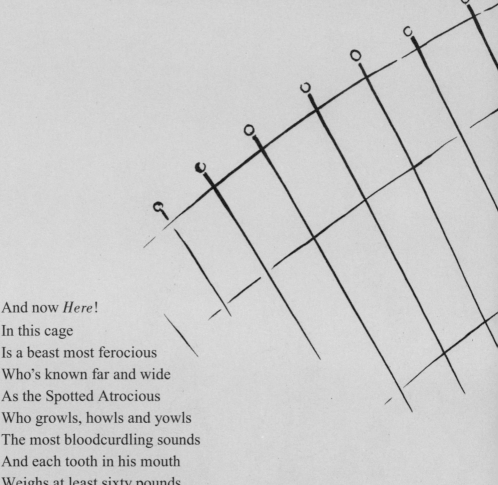

And now *Here*!
In this cage
Is a beast most ferocious
Who's known far and wide
As the Spotted Atrocious
Who growls, howls and yowls
The most bloodcurdling sounds
And each tooth in his mouth
Weighs at least sixty pounds
And he chews up and eats with the greatest of ease
Things like carpets and sidewalks and people and trees!
But the great Colonel Sneelock is just the right kind
Of a man who can tame him. I'm sure he won't mind.

　　快瞧这儿!这个笼子里住的是世界上最凶猛的动物——斑点兽,他低吼、嚎叫、咆哮,声音令人毛骨悚然,他的牙齿每颗至少有六十磅重,他可以轻而易举地吃掉地毯、人行道、行人和树木!但是,伟大的斯尼洛克上校恰好能驯服他。我确信他不会介意。

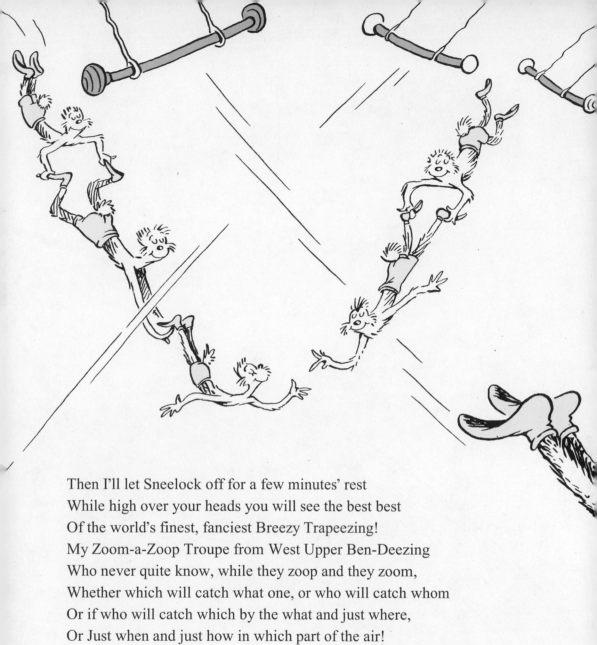

Then I'll let Sneelock off for a few minutes' rest
While high over your heads you will see the best best
Of the world's finest, fanciest Breezy Trapeezing!
My Zoom-a-Zoop Troupe from West Upper Ben-Deezing
Who never quite know, while they zoop and they zoom,
Whether which will catch what one, or who will catch whom
Or if who will catch which by the what and just where,
Or Just when and just how in which part of the air!

　　接下来，我想让斯尼洛克退场休息几分钟。大家抬起头，可以欣赏到世界上最精彩、最奇特的空中飞人表演！我的"上下翻飞剧团"来自西北本兹，没人知道他们在上下翻飞的时候，哪个会抓住哪个，谁会抓住谁，谁会在哪儿抓住谁的哪个部位，或者什么时候在空中的什么地方怎样抓住。

Ei! Ei! What a circus! My Circus McGurkus!
My workers love work. They say, "Work us! Please work us!
We'll work and we'll work up so many surprises
You'd never see half if you had forty eyses!"

噢！噢！多棒的马戏团啊！我的麦格克斯马戏团！我的员工热爱工作。他们说："让我工作！请让我工作！我们愿意工作！我们会弄出很多花样，即使你有四十只眼睛也忙不过来。"

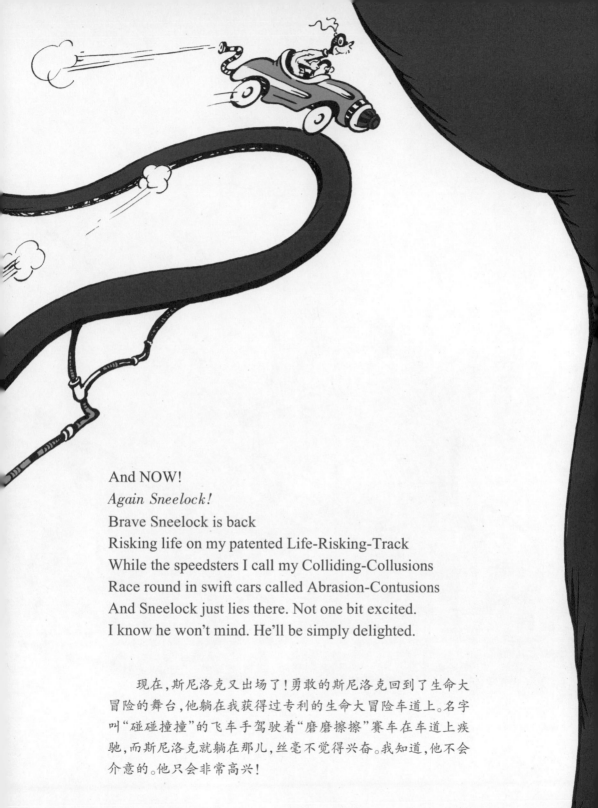

And NOW!
Again Sneelock!
Brave Sneelock is back
Risking life on my patented Life-Risking-Track
While the speedsters I call my Colliding-Collusions
Race round in swift cars called Abrasion-Contusions
And Sneelock just lies there. Not one bit excited.
I know he won't mind. He'll be simply delighted.

　　现在,斯尼洛克又出场了!勇敢的斯尼洛克回到了生命大
冒险的舞台,他躺在我获得过专利的生命大冒险车道上。名字
叫"碰碰撞撞"的飞车手驾驶着"磨磨擦擦"赛车在车道上疾
驰,而斯尼洛克就躺在那儿,丝毫不觉得兴奋。我知道,他不会
介意的。他只会非常高兴!

And *here,* in a contest of brute-strength and muscle,
Kid Sneelock, my champ-of-all-champs, will now tussle
And wrestle a beast called the Grizzly-Ghastly
And slap him around! Then he'll slam him down fastly
And pin both his shoulders tight flat to the mat.
Kid Sneelock will love it! I'm sure about that.

　　这儿正在进行力量的角逐，小斯尼洛克和最强大的冠军现在
要展开较量，他会将他打倒在地，把他的肩膀紧紧按在垫子上。小
斯尼洛克会喜欢的，我对此深信不疑。

And while THAT goes on THERE, look at THIS go on HERE!
Have you heard of my herd of "Through-Horns-Jumping-Deer"...?
Every deer jumps through horns of another pell-mell
While his horns are jumped through at the same time as well
By a deer whose horns ALSO are being jumped through
By another who's having HIS horns jumped through, too,
Which I'm *sure* Trainer Sneelock can train them to do.

　　在那边精彩节目上演的同时，来看看这边的绝妙演出吧。听说过我的"在鹿角之间蹦跳的鹿群"吗……?每一只鹿都从另一只鹿的鹿角之间蹦过去,同时又有别的鹿又从他的鹿角之间蹦过去,而那只从他的鹿角之间蹦过去的鹿的鹿角之间还有别的鹿跳过。我相信驯兽师斯尼洛克能训练他们做到这一点。

Then the whole tent will ring with hoorays and wild shouts
When I wheel in my whales and they turn on their spouts!
First my Whale Number One, with an aim that aims true
Spouts a spout that spouts Sneelock to Whale Number Two!
And then Whale Number Two spouts his spout like a gun
And that spout spouts old Sneelock right back to Whale One!
And then forwards and backwards on spout after spout
My great Spout-Rider Sneelock gets spouted about
Just as long as the water they're spouting holds out!

　　当被我推上舞台的鲸鱼打开他们的喷水孔时，整个帐篷里欢呼声尖叫声响成一片！首先出场的是一号鲸鱼，他喷出的水柱瞄得很准，能正好把斯尼洛克射到二号鲸鱼的喷水孔上！然后，二号鲸鱼喷出的水柱像枪一样，将老斯尼洛克稳稳送回一号鲸鱼那里。他们你喷一下，我喷一下，过去又回来。斯尼洛克是个了不起的水柱骑手，只要鲸鱼能喷出水，他就总是可以被喷来喷去。

Then my Tournament Knights! Noble apes without fears!
Sir Hector! Sir Vector! Sir Bopps! And Sir Beers!
Sir Hawkins! Sir Dawkins! Sir Jawks! And Sir Jeers!
Clatter into the tent, and while everyone cheers
Stage a roust-about-joust with their boxing glove spears!

　　随后出场的是我的联赛骑士!他们是勇敢无畏的猩猩——赫克托爵士!维克多爵士!波普斯爵士!比尔斯爵士!霍金斯爵士!道金斯爵士!基尔斯爵士!他们卡嗒卡嗒地走进帐篷,在观众的欢呼声中登上舞台,手持戴拳击手套的长矛,表演了激动人心的骑马大战。

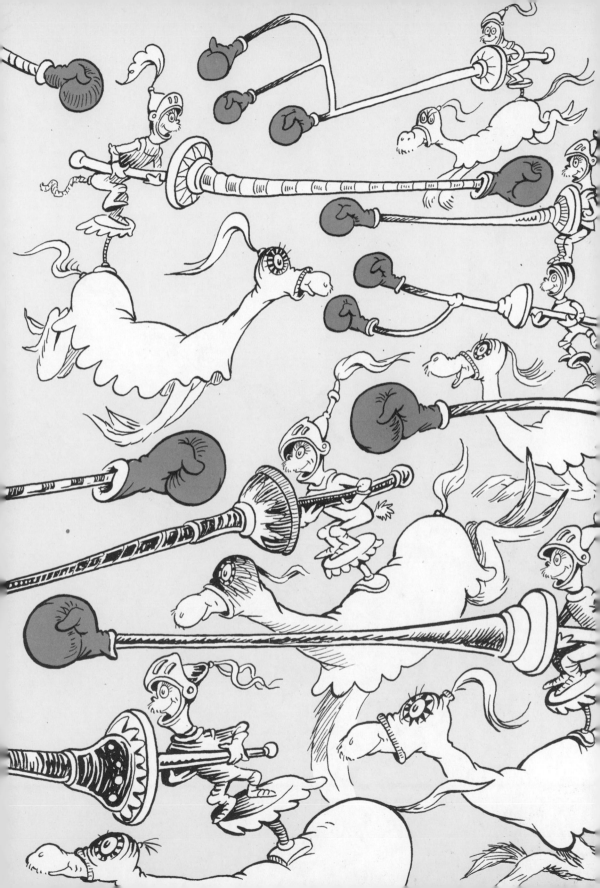

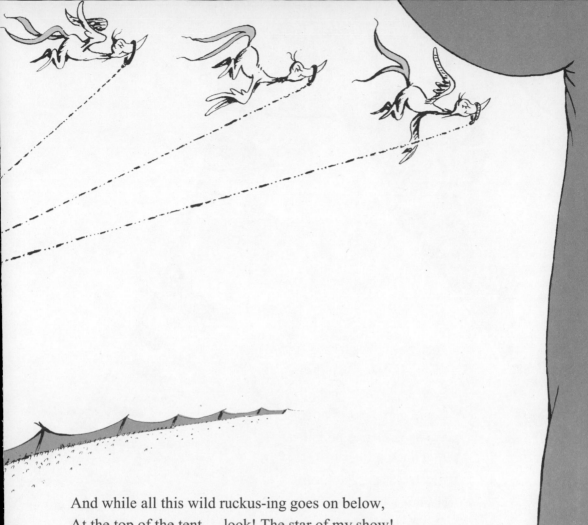

And while all this wild ruckus-ing goes on below,
At the top of the tent. . . look! The star of my show!
Great Daredevil Sneelock! The world's bravest type!
He comes pulled through the air by three Soobrian Snipe
On a dingus contraption attached to his pipe!
And while people below are all turning chalk white
And all biting their fingernails off in their fright,
Great Sneelock soars up to a terrible height!

　　底下狂野的喧闹声经久不息,而在帐篷顶上……快看呀!本场的明星来了!天不怕地不怕的斯尼洛克!世界上最勇敢的人!三只苏恩沙锥鸟拉着挂在他烟斗上的小玩意儿,带他在空中盘旋!下面的观众吓得脸色煞白,紧紧咬着自己的指甲,看,伟大的斯尼洛克正飞向惊人的高度!

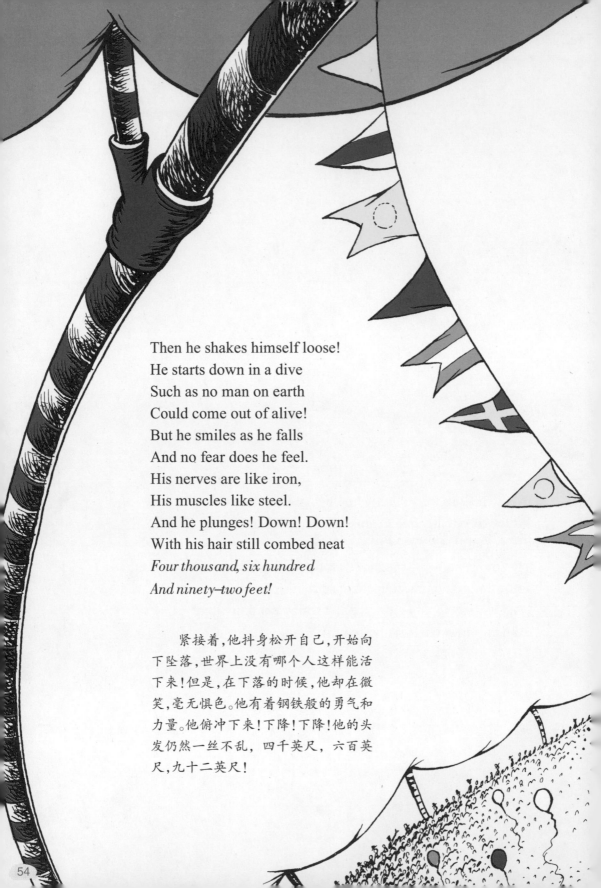

Then he shakes himself loose!
He starts down in a dive
Such as no man on earth
Could come out of alive!
But he smiles as he falls
And no fear does he feel.
His nerves are like iron,
His muscles like steel.
And he plunges! Down! Down!
With his hair still combed neat
Four thousand, six hundred
And ninety-two feet!

　　紧接着,他抖身松开自己,开始向
下坠落,世界上没有哪个人这样能活
下来!但是,在下落的时候,他却在微
笑,毫无惧色。他有着钢铁般的勇气和
力量。他俯冲下来!下降!下降!他的头
发仍然一丝不乱,四千英尺,六百英
尺,九十二英尺!

Then he'll land in a fish bowl.
He'll manage just fine.
Don't ask *how* he'll manage.
That's *his* job. Not mine.

然后，他落在了一个鱼缸里，他
能做得恰到好处。别问我他怎么能
做到，那是他的事儿，不是我的。

SNEELOCK'S STORE

啊哈!他会成为一个大英雄!
等他发现身后冒出一个大马戏团,
他当然不会介意。

Why! He'll be a Hero!
Of *course* he won't mind
When he finds that he has
A big circus behind.

阅读提示

这是一场想象的盛宴，是男孩麦格克关于他的麦格克斯马戏团的一场狂野的想象。

不错，麦格克斯马戏团属于男孩麦格克。因为，这个驾轻就熟地提供了一连串"世界上最伟大表演"的马戏团，这个空前绝后的马戏团，全出自他的想象。

小麦格克的想象并非没有立足点：他有一个绝妙的场地——斯尼洛克商店后面的一大片空地，和一个绝不会有辱使命的合作者——商店的主人斯尼洛克先生，所以他从未视他的马戏团为想象，而是称之为"我的宏伟计划"。从一开始这小主人公就气魄宏大，很轻松地认为即使这片空地上有棵枯树和两三辆破汽车，他也完全能够在半个小时之内完成清理工作，接着本书一气呵成的精彩故事就在他的想入非非推动之下迅速拉开了帷幕，并水到渠成地冲向高潮。

马戏团首演之夜节目的神奇、惊险、玄妙，也是本书故事情节的神奇、惊险、玄妙，更乃苏斯博士想象力之神奇、惊险、玄妙，这些处处来源于细节的魅力，显示了细节的力量，这也正是苏斯博士的艺术创造力——包括故事的编织和画面的构图与表现——之天才独特过人之处。比如海狮鲁尔夫竟能以一根胡须支撑倒立在五个小球的顶上；比如蒙眼神箭手那根一路辗转穿越了八道怪异关卡的箭最终射穿的是放在斯尼洛克头顶上的一颗山楂，而不是常见的苹果；最有趣的是斯尼洛克。麦格克从让他做点儿小事、帮点儿小忙开始而一发不可收拾,接二连三地赋予其超凡的能力;而斯尼洛克纵然历尽千惊万险也始终是闭着双眼、叼着烟斗、趿拉着拖鞋,连头发也一丝不乱。直到本书最后一幅画面,一向气定神闲的他突然双目圆睁,仿佛一场酣梦猛醒,苏斯博士也就此给他这个热烈响亮的狂欢故事打上了一个漂亮的休止符。

儿童文学博士　李　虹